THE
LITTLE
RED
DRAGON

P1

THE
LITTLE
RED
DRAGON

by ESTELLE URBAHNS

pictures by WEDA YAP

E. P. DUTTON & CO., INC. · NEW YORK · 1947

THE LITTLE RED DRAGON is dedicated to the principal, teachers, and pupils of the Newton Booth School, Sacramento, California, in appreciation of their portrayal of THE TANGLED WEB by an exquisite shadow play enacted by the pupils.

THE LITTLE RED DRAGON

A night watchman, threading his way along Pottery-Making Street, struck his musical gong and called lustily, "It is the Hour of the Dog and eastward blows the wind."

Chang, the Potter, and his adopted son, Chang Fen, were closing the panels of the shop. Though Chang's words sometimes cut like the lash of a bamboo whipping-rod, his voice was gentle as he turned to the boy and spoke behind his hand, "O-yo! Limping One, the Hour of the Dog brings darkness at this time of year, and the young moon has set. Therefore, since no curious eye can now watch what we do, I shall take you into the garden back of my shop, for you must learn where my ancient treasures

9

are buried. The one which is concealed in my garden path beneath the ninth flagstone, I treasure above all my hidden possessions. I would have you see it. This night I would teach you how to take it from its secret place in the earth, for you are now my son."

At the words, "my son" the boy again recalled how his former family name had been changed from Lui to Chang, for, since his adoption by the potter nine moons ago, he was no longer Lui Fen, but was now Chang Fen, and his full name would continue to be Chang Fen all the remaining days that he lived.

Would Shou Tao, the smiling God-Of-Long-Life, give him many years in which to bring honor to the house of his foster father? He must remember to ask this favor each night as he knelt at the altar table just before creeping beneath his silk *pu-gai*, which covered him like a warm protecting wing.

"Come, my son," Chang whispered, "let us go. But first we shall remove our sandals, for at this hour even the garden walls may have ears."

The heart of young Fen was beating high as he placed his sandals by the paneled door, for adventure was calling from the dark little garden. Soon he was to see the hidden treasure, cherished above all others by his foster father. Was he worthy to be entrusted with such a secret?

"We shall take four steps to the right, my son, then five steps toward the ancient plum tree," whispered Chang.

"This will bring us to the ninth flagstone. Walk softly as a cat!"

Though his steps were light as moving shadows, Chang Fen tingled with happy excitement from his closely-cropped head to the toes of his bare feet, for mystery, like floating incense, seemed to fill the garden.

All at once the potter stood still. "We have reached the ninth flagstone," he whispered.

In the stillness, Chang Fen could hear him brushing leaves from the ancient stone. The potter now drew the boy's hand downward until it touched an iron ring. It seemed to him as large around as his tea bowl.

"There are two such rings," Chang explained, his lips close to the boy's ear. "They are fixed to either side of the flagstone, yet lie so well hidden in the flowering moss of the garden path that no eye can see them. Now grasp both rings, my son, and then try to lift the stone to which they are attached."

Ai-ya! Here, indeed, was a challenge to young strength!

Though he had a lame foot that dragged slightly when he walked, Chang Fen's arms, shoulders, and back were whole and strong. He knew a fine pride in the strength of his arms, and he longed to have his foster father equally proud of this strength. Perhaps some day, he, young Fen, might bring honor to the house of Chang by the work of his hands and arms. Ai! The potter might then forget entirely that his son limped as they walked together on feast days along the avenues of over-hanging willows—

"Come!" Chang urged sharply. "Try to lift the stone and then swing it to one side."

Chang Fen bent eagerly to the task, pulling with all his might against the weight of the stone. The iron rings bit into his fingers. Had the flagstone grown fast to the earth?

"Come! Give more of your strength," Chang pleaded under his breath, "for, remember, he who cannot overcome small difficulties can never achieve greatness."

His heart yearning to obey the potter's command, Fen by slow inches pulled the stone from the earth and then swung it to one side.

"It is a task well done," murmured Chang.

In the darkness, the boy sank to the ground, panting for breath, but his heart was singing, because once again, the honorable Chang had been pleased with the son of his choice.

By starlight, young Fen could make out a square opening in the earth. "In this dark recess," Chang whispered, "my best-loved treasure lies hidden from thieves."

Thieves! Limping One mused over the word.

"Other craftsmen in Pottery-Making Street would give for my treasure many taels* in pure silver," Chang continued. "But besides myself, only you, Son of my House, know of this hiding place, and no one would suspect it.

* Tael—Chinese weight equaling about one and one-third ounce.

"Now stretch your fingers into the black opening until you touch a box of bronze," Chang commanded softly. "Then lift the box and carry it without a sound into the shop."

Ai-ya! Again the word rushed to the boy's lips, but he closed them against it. Here was yet another challenge for Chang's adopted son! Could he obey the command without a sound or without a clumsy step which listening ears beyond the garden wall might overhear? If only his lame foot would not cause him to stumble!

CHAPTER 2

His hands could be trusted, Chang Fen assured himself, for often he had proved them to be dependable as well as painstaking. Nine moons ago had he not mended, worthy of Chang's approval, the shattered lid of Perfect Little Teapot?

"Do as I command!" ordered the potter, his lips once again close to the boy's ear. "Lift the box from the dark opening and then carry it without a sound into the shop."

Young Fen reached into the cavity. His fingers touched the box of bronze. He found it cold as the Wintry Breath of the Dragon. Grasping the box, he lifted it as gently as a mother might lift her baby from its cradle.

With slow care the boy then moved toward the shop, feeling his way with bare toes. The flagstones were cold against his feet. Now the Rain Goddess was looping cloud

15

veils across the stars, thus causing the little garden to seem black as a cave. A whispered hope quivered on the boy's lips: if only his lame foot would not cause him to stumble———

Presently, through the latticed windows of the shop, young Fen could see a faint glow from the vegetable oil lamp. A few more careful steps and the paneled door would be reached!

Ai! The word sang in his thumping heart when finally he stepped within the back room of the shop. The next moment, Fen could hear Chang bolting the door and then fastening the iron grille across the moon-window.

Lips parted, eyes unblinking, Chang Fen watched as the potter arranged a screen and stools about the square red table with its vegetable oil lamp. Now, lifting the box from the boy's hands, Chang placed it near the light, murmuring, "Here, my son, no curious eye can see as we gaze upon my treasure."

Though Limping One sat quiet as a stone image, happy puzzlement welled in his heart. What manner of thing lay in the little box! He held his breath as Chang removed the lid. With hands that trembled slightly, the man then lifted from the box a slim scroll of silk, fragrant with musk, and he said, "Though the silk is light as air, it is, neverthe-less, sturdy as a leaf of bamboo. Touch it, my son."

The boy knew a thrill of pleasure as he smoothed the scroll with a fingertip. When spread upon the table, he discovered that the bit of silk appeared no larger than a lady's handkerchief. Painted on it was a crane, a plum tree, and the moon. As he gazed at the picture, the boy's eyes shone as with a light, for surely spirit hands had painted it!

"By your face it is plain that you are delighted by the Crane-Moon-And-Plum-Tree design," murmured Chang. "That is well, for now you are my son. Listen with care, and I shall tell you an ancient tale."

First the potter reached into his sleeve pocket, drawing forth a bit of carved red jade. It was the little red dragon! Chang Fen caught his breath at sight of the stone, for, at other times, he had seen the potter take it from his sleeve pocket. Fascinated, the boy saw again how the crystal eyes of the little dragon winked and glowed in the lamplight. As he watched, Chang, in his usual way, rubbed his thumb over the bit of jade as he talked, and the story flowed smoothly:

"Listen with care, my son, to the tale of the silk scroll. Two thousand moons ago (161 years) my illustrious ancestor, Chang Mao, painted this honorable Crane-Moon-And-Plum-Tree design with his own brush pen. He was certain that the design had been given to him by the kindly gods, for the ancient potter saw it one night in a dream. He arose quickly from his tile bed and painted this loveliness before he could forget any part of it."

Still rubbing his thumb over the little red dragon, Chang was silent for a moment; then, "Because this painting

came thus from the gods, its use was not intended for the earning of mere silver. So, once in every generation, a descendant of the House of Chang—a youth—is chosen to make a ceremonial urn. The urn is then baked to the color of an autumn peach. Lastly, the heaven-sent design is painted on the urn. If the work is done without flaw, the urn is then carried to the temple beyond the moon gate. There it is humbly offered as a ceremonial piece for holding the honorable joss-sticks."

The story was told. Returning the little red dragon to his sleeve pocket, Chang reached across the table and grasping the hands of his adopted son held them in his own. "Limping One," he said gently, "you were favored at birth with beauty-making fingers. Since you are now Son of the House of Chang, and because you are fast learning the use of the potter's wheel, you shall before long fashion an urn of white kaolin. You shall then bake the urn to the color of an autumn peach. After that—who can tell——?"

At the hint of promise back of the words, Chang Fen's heart leaped. Could it be that Chang was planning one day to permit him, Fen, to copy the heaven-sent design? Could such honor, perchance, ever come to him, who so recently had been a penniless orphan? The mere thought sent a glow of happiness from fingers to toes.

The boy gazed at his slender hands as though seeing them for the first time, and he mused over the words, "beauty-making fingers." With such fingers might he create beauty lovely enough for temple use? If so, then the day might come when his honorable foster father could forget that his son limped. Beauty-making fingers might of themselves bring honor to the House of Chang. This, after all, was the most important thing to do, for had not Chang brought him, Fen, when hungry and homeless, out of the cold one night, as he lay against Hankow's great wall? Had not Chang fed him and given him a good bed of tile and heated bricks, a leather pillow, and a warm *pu-gai* for a cover? In addition, nine moons ago, the honorable Chang had adopted him, a crippled boy, and made him his son.

All at once, Limping One thought of Meng, the oldest apprentice, who was an orphan. Meng possessed unusual skill in tracing designs. But his unfriendly eyes seemed daily to ask of Fen, "Why was I not chosen, in place of you, as Son of the House of Chang?" If Meng were given the chance, could he excel him, young Fen, in copying the ancient design? Limping One thrust the idea aside.

Once again the night watchman, threading his way along Pottery-Making Street, struck his musical gong and called lustily, "It is the Hour of the Pig and the Rain Goddess is tapping on the earth."

"Now you must sleep, Son of my House," said Chang. "While I return the box to its hiding place, get quickly onto thy warm tile bed."

As young Fen was drifting into sleep, he again wondered

if he were worthy to be trusted with a secret as great as the one which had been told him this night. Would he remember not to whisper about it in Pottery-Making Street?

But he dreamed of the little red dragon with its crystal eyes, knowing that he would feel like a real son of the house of Chang if he might carry such a treasure in his own sleeve pocket——

A week later Chang called his adopted son to the back room and said, "Every year before Frozen Dew comes to the fields, I leave the shop and cross the river Han to visit my respected sister, Lu Chee. From her little inland farm I may gaze upon flowering valleys and hear the rice birds singing in the paddies. There, for a season, I can rest my old bones.

"In past times," Chang continued, "my revered cousin, Lao, has cared for the shop in my absence. But now I have a son!" the potter added proudly. "Therefore, in your hands, Son of my House, I leave everything."

"I—I hear you, my father." Chang Fen bowed low. "Nothing will I neglect."

Happiness welled in the boy's heart, for Chang was

trusting his chosen son to care for one of the busiest shops in Pottery-Making Street, trusting him with his most cherished hidden possession. To be worthy of such trust was a high challenge to courage and wits!

The next morning after rice and tea, the potter again pulled the bit of carved jade from his sleeve pocket. He then slipped it into his new son's hand, declaring, "It pleases me to leave with you my Jade One."

As sight of the red stone, shaped like a dragon, once again the boy's face glowed. He watched fascinated as the crystal eyes winked and sparkled in the light.

"I call it my charm piece," said Chang, "for it has brought me good luck." He smiled whimsically. "Always it goes with me wherever I go. Nevertheless, I leave my red Jade One with you, Son of my House, as a small companion while I am away."

A charm piece! Intrigued, young Fen mused over the word. Might not the mere holding of the bit of carved jade, shaped like a dragon, give new working magic to his fingers? In the event that Chang might permit his adopted son to copy the Crane-Moon-And-Plum-Tree design, would the charm piece bring him good luck in this difficult task? A fine pride encircled the heart of Fen as he cradled the little red dragon in his hands, for it would seem that his foster father was learning to trust him as he would trust a real son.

Was not the valuable bit of jade left for his pleasure a proof of this?

"On the seventh day, when the shadow of my plum tree lies eastward across the garden, I shall return," said Chang, breaking into the boy's thought. The next moment he stepped into a waiting ricksha.

The days that followed were busy ones, and young Fen's heart was filled with a great happiness. His light step told of it and his face shone with it.

Meng, the oldest apprentice, with his unfriendly eyes and sure feet, still carried the tea basket into the shop, where he served the hot drink, flavored with dried jasmine flowers, to Chang's most important customers. But young Fen, Son of the House, had been entrusted with the highest service, for he stood behind the counter, displaying bowls, plates, and cups to the best advantage. As the customers lingered over the bargaining, the boy rubbed his thumb over the red dragon, finding that this helped to smooth his bits of conversation with older heads. And each day he asked himself: would holding the charm piece in his hands give a new working-magic to his fingers?

Each evening, with an empty gourd, he ladled rain water from the leaf-green jar, and then poured it over the garden beds, soaking them thoroughly as Chang had taught him to do. He kept a sharp eye on Lo Lu, the accountant, whose fingers moved fleetly over the counting-board every time a sale was made. Moreover, the boy saw that each day's earnings of silver and copper taels were locked safely in the wall panel of the inner room.

Every morning, as he watched Meng and Chi wash and strain the clay to free it from small pebbles and bits of root, young Fen was glad that no longer was he required to do this lowly task. For six moons Chang had permitted him to work at the potter's wheel, whose humming sound always seemed like the whirring of cranes' wings against the sky. As he worked at the wheel, in Chang's absence, fashioning tea bowls that were smooth as lotus petals, the boy once again pondered over the words, "beauty-making fingers." Would he be able one day to fashion an urn fit for temple use——?

During the potter's absence, young Fen dreaded the nights; for, after Meng and Chi were asleep on the flat roof, he drove himself to carry his bed mat and *pu-gai* into the cold garden. There, curled over the ninth flagstone, he lay half waking through the black hours.

On the sixth night he started up in panic at a sound near the garden wall. *Ai-ya!* Had a thief, learning of Chang's absence, come searching for possible treasure? If so, might he carry a—weapon?

Suddenly a tempting thought came to young Fen. In his bare feet, he could easily creep unheard back into the shop. There, behind a bolted door, he would be safe as a

mouse under a broom. But the next moment he remembered the painting. The design on the silk had been heaven-sent, so it was believed. Chang loved the beautiful scroll above all his hidden possessions. Young Fen made his decision. Though only a boy of thirteen years and nine moons, he would remain in the garden and struggle to the last breath, if need be, to save Chang's treasure.

Again came the sound of a step crunching over dry leaves. Other steps followed. Did he fancy it, or were the steps coming toward the ninth flagstone? Had the intruder in some way learned of Chang's best-loved hidden treasure——?

Swiftly gathering his wits, the boy remembered how the Bread Seller, in passing along Pottery-Making Street, shouted into his cupped hands to make his voice sound like that of three men. Perhaps in this way, he, Chang Fen, could frighten the intruder——

His heart lurching until it shook his body, young Fen cupped his hands about his mouth and called into the darkness, "*Begone from the garden of Chang! Begone or I shall call the night watchman!*"

Now there came a rustling sound in the ancient vine that grew on the wall. A moment later, young Fen could make out a figure in the starlight. It was slipping over the mud wall. Suddenly it was gone.

Relief soothing as rain settled in the boy's heart, but

the next moment he was asking himself in renewed panic: might the intruder return————?

At the thought, floods of strength seemed to flow into the boy's arms as he groped in the darkness for the iron rings. Now grasping them he tugged at the flagstone with all his might. Once again the iron rings bit into his fingers. But at last the heavy stone was pulled from the earth. Once more his strong arms had won!

The boy stopped to listen, but there was no sound in the garden. Nevertheless, he must work quickly, he told his thumping heart. Reaching into the cavity, with deft fingers he removed the lid from the bronze box, and then with delicate touch lifted from it the painting which was light as air, yet sturdy as a leaf of bamboo. He slipped the scroll of silk into his cloth girdle. Soundlessly replacing the lid, with straining arms he lowered the flagstone.

Rising from his knees, the boy stood for a moment, dread tearing at his heart. At least, if he were to meet the prowler, the man would find nothing in the hands of Chang's son. Again the boy listened, but all was still in the garden. Ai-ya! Could he make his way to the shop without mishap?

The boy moved with slow care, feeling his way with bare toes. A whispered hope quivered on his lips: if only his lame foot would not cause him to fall and perhaps rumple the little silk scroll!

"*Ai!Ai!*" he breathed joyously when at last he reached the paneled door, and then slid the bolt into place. With unhurried care, he drew the silk painting from his girdle. It was unharmed, *safe!*

How glad his revered father would be when he learned the story! *Ai!* Once more he might be pleased with his new son! At the thought, joy encircled the heart of Limping One.

The boy formed a plan as he made his way to the inner room. He would roll the priceless scrap of silk on a brush pen, and then slip the brush pen into the hollow bamboo whipping rod. What thief——even though he were to enter the shop and search the inner room——would think of looking into a whipping rod for treasure! A triumphant smile curved the boy's lips.

"*Ai!Ai!Ai-i-i!*" In joy over such rare service to his thrice-honorable father, the words made a little song. As young Fen burst into the inner room, the silk scroll held high above his head, his face was aglow. "*Ai! Ai! Ai-i-i!*" he exclaimed again in breathless excitement.

Abruptly, however, the singing words were hushed, for a man holding a lamp stood in the room. His shadow cast by the light was stretched large and black on the wall behind him. The man was——Chang! For some reason he had returned a day early from the little inland farm.

A joyous word rushed to the boy's lips. He was about

to lift the ancient scroll higher still and tell what things had happened. Instead, an exclamation of dismay quivered in the boy's throat, for the potter's face appeared hard and frozen as a lake in the twelfth moon.

Placing the lamp on the table, Chang, with swooping fingers, reached for the scroll, lifting it with infinite care from the boy's hands, and at the same time hissing, "So-o-o! While my face was turned away, you, whom I chose for my son, would attempt to carry off the sacred possession of an ancestor! *Ai-ya!* No doubt you have planned to sell this treasure of the House of Chang in Pottery-Making Street for many taels of silver! Bah!"

"No-o-o-o!" The word was like a sob. "Give——give heart, Honorable One! Only let me tell——!"

"*Silence!* Did I not see the look of greed making bright your eyes when you broke into this room, waving like a flag the sacred scroll? Did I not hear you gloating over it with singing lips? This did I both see and hear!"

Chang's voice shook. To Limping One, who stood trembling, it sounded like the rolling drums of the Thunder God. Just above a whisper, the boy again ventured an explanation, "I——I am innocent, Revered One."

"I *command* you to silence!" roared Chang. "Does not a robber always shout of his innocence!" The potter held out the scroll, declaring, "*Here is the evidence!* Moreover, guilt has made your face whiter than bean curd. It has also caused your words to stumble. Fortunate it is that I returned this night in time to save my most cherished possession!"

Young Fen made still another daring attempt to speak. The words tangled in his throat. He now realized in bleak despair that everything that the eye could see did tell of guilt. If only the angry potter would look into his new son's heart, there he would find the truth!

But Chang, in his blind anger, did not trouble to look into his new son's heart. Instead, quick feet carried him to the door panel. He was now unlocking the panel, now pushing it noisomely to one side.

Watching open-mouthed, bewildered, panic began to well into the heart of Limping One, for memory of the grim days when he had roamed shivering and hungry along the streets of Hankow now came crowding back upon him. At this moment, night, through the open door panel, appeared deep and black as a cave. Its breath, cold, damp, and hostile, seemed to rush against him.

As the boy drew back a step into the warm room, Chang's voice thundered: "Since you have betrayed my deep trust in you, because you have been guilty of the most shameful offense: profaning with dirty fingers* *the treasure of an ancestor,* I now cast you into the street. Go!"

* Stealing hands.

"But I have done no wrong! I am innocent!" cried young Fen, his voice breaking in a final daring attempt to clear himself.

Chang, however, face grim, stood unmoved, a long finger pointing into the night. "Go!" he repeated.

The word fell like a cudgel against the face and body of Limping One and sank burning into his heart. Had Meng, on his roof bed, heard all and smiled? Meng, whose unfriendly eyes seemed daily to ask, "Why was *I* not chosen, instead of you, as Son of the House of Chang?"

For a moment, the boy's glance lingered about the inner room. Here, in this place of comfort, the Honorable Chang and he had spent their evenings. Here, the potter had told him stories of the ancients. Here, by the square red table, he was learning to brush characters so that one day he could both read and write.

The boy peered into his own chamber with its tile bed. The bricks beneath the tile were heated in winter, making it warm as a tea basket. On the wall hung a scroll painting of butterflies. Young Fen recalled that the butterfly stands for joy. Chang, who was sometimes called Lover of Beautiful Things, had hung the painting. Chang had been learning to trust his new son. Perhaps even to——love him a little——

By the jars of the water clock, Fen could see that the

hour was nearing midnight. The wind was rattling the panels of the shop. Limping One backed slowly from the inner room, murmuring to its emptiness, "I——I go, Revered One, and——and I take with me a small heart."

CHAPTER 4

As the boy stepped into the autumn night, a feeling of desolation sank into his already small heart. He was certain that the Rain Goddess was riding in the air just above him, for her cool gray sleeves were brushing his forehead. Would she soon be dashing silver beads of water full upon him? *Ai-ya!* Where in all Hankow could he go this night? He recalled bleakly the good tile bed left behind in the rear of Chang's shop.

Rickshas were moving through the street, carrying passengers from theater and tea house. Young Fen drew his outer coat high about his neck, and watched late stragglers with lanterns padding through the dark. Again he wondered despairingly in what direction to turn his sandalled feet.

A blind beggar passed, striking up a wistful melody on

his bamboo tubes. A rush of pity crowding into his heart, Chang Fen gazed after the man. They were like brothers, he decided, for neither he nor the beggar had a warm place in which to lie.

After a time the boy discovered a sheltered doorway, and crept into its deep shadow. Sleep came at last, and Limping One dreamed of the honorable Chang to whom unwittingly he had brought sorrow. "Anything would I do to help lift up his heart again," he boy murmured, half waking.

Finally a great din from Brass-Pounding Street told that early morning had come. Dawn's pale light brought coolies with swinging baskets. Trotting briskly by the sheltered doorway in which young Fen sat crouched, they chanted the age-old rhythm of work, *"Hi-ya-ho! Hi-ya-ho!"*

An hour passed. Foot-passengers began to crowd the narrow street-way. Now came a bean cake peddler, twanging a stick against his metal gong and shouting his wares. Presently, came housewives, being pushed to market in sturdy wheelbarrows. A peddler, with food heated by a small stove beneath his cart, passed so close to Chang Fen that he could catch the odor of hot pork dumplings. But the ache in his heart was greater far than the ache of his hunger. *Chang had thought him guilty of theft!* The boy turned away from the cart of food and stepped into the moving throng of people.

With the foot passengers, he moved aimlessly into

Umbrella-Making Street. Mid morning came. Again he stood in a doorway, wondering which way to go.

The next moment panic chilled the heart of Limping One, for he was aware that a man with a pock-marked face was studying him from across the street-way. Young Fen saw that the man wore a cap with a blue button. In terror, the boy wondered if *yung* was painted on the back of the stranger's coat. If so, then the pock-marked one was a ya-men runner! Had he been sent by the magistrate, at the potter's request, to bring him, young Fen, to prison? His terror mounting, the boy fancied he could not move.

Closer came the man. There was purpose in his step.

All at once young Fen dropped to his hands and knees by the side of a fuel carrier who was bearing huge bundles of mountain grass. Creeping beside him, the boy made a twisting way to right and left among the hurrying crowd. Suddenly he bumped against the chair of a workman, who was painting umbrellas at the door of his shop.

"O Umbrella-Maker! Hide me!" pleaded the boy, still crouching low. "I ask it in the name of kind heaven!"

"Are the ya-men runners in pursuit that you must crawl on the ground, my son?" asked the worker, dipping his brush into red lacquer.

Prostrate at the man's feet, Chang Fen told his plight in whispered snatches.

"I am convinced that you speak the truth," the umbrella-maker declared, "for the words fall from your lips as

naturally as water from a spring. Here! Quickly! Creep behind this newly-painted umbrella, and you will be as snugly hidden as a cocoon beneath a mulberry leaf. In place of morning rice, here is a sugared plum," added the man, pulling the sweetmeat from his belt.

Since the ache in his heart was still greater than the pain of his hunger, young Fen dropped the sugared plum into his sleeve pocket.

After midday, the umbrella-maker touched the boy on the shoulder. "Hasten!" he whispered, "Cross the street to the farmer in his two-wheeled cart with its painted chest. Look! He now turns his Mongolian pony toward the city gates. This means that his chest of melons is sold and that he is about to return to his land. Go to him and say that his good friend, Ling, the Umbrella-Maker, asks if you with the lame foot may ride with him to the country where you may earn your rice and tea."

Thanking Ling in a rush of whispered words, Chang Fen, still crouching low, scurried toward the two-wheeled cart. A few moments later, he lay curled in the straw-lined chest.

As the cart began to wind through the narrow streets, the heart of Limping One beat in terror. Had the man with the blue button on his cap seen him, young Fen, creep into the painted chest? Was the stranger following the cart? Peeping through the cracks in the chest, the boy's eyes darted from right to left over the moving crowd. Breathlessly he watched as the cart threaded its way over a bridge, finally swinging through the city gates. "Ai! Ai-i-i!" the boy murmured at last. Heaven had watched over him——one of China's lesser ones——for the pock-marked man, with the blue button on his cap, was nowhere to be seen.

CHAPTER 5

Country air began to sift through the cracks in the painted chest. While the sun moved down the sky, young Fen slept. He did not awaken until a hand touched his shoulder, causing him to cry out with renewed terror. But he saw that only the kindly farmer was peering into the chest.

"I have reached my poor land," he explained. "Half a li westward lives the farmer, Win. He may have work for you to do. Good fortune attend you, my son."

Scrambling from the two-wheeled cart, Chang Fen bowed three times before the man. "Respected Sir," he murmured, "not in ten summers and winters shall I forget your kindness."

Glancing about, the boy saw bean fields, willow banks, a river winding, and a boatman in a tiny barge singing against the wind. Cranes flew in the amber light of evening. The air was sweet.

"*Ai!*" Young Fen murmured, his heart gladdening for a moment. To work in such a place for rice and tea would be good! Here, in the country, surely the man with the blue on his cap would not find him! After a time, here he could forget that the potter carried an angry mind against him. *Ai!* Here, at the end of a single moon, his heart might grow happy and content!

As young Fen set out for the house of Win, his hunger seemed nearly as great as the pain in his heart. He reached into his sleeve pocket for the sugared plum. The next moment, however, a cry burst from him, for his fingers had touched the little red dragon. Thoughts in a turmoil, he pulled from his pocket the bit of carved jade, and gazed at it with stricken face. In the evening light, the dragon's tiny crystal eyes sparkled like living eyes. In sharp dismay, the boy remembered there was a certain magic in the little red dragon, for was it not a charm piece? One which had brought luck to the honorable Chang? At this moment was Chang missing it? Was the potter, Lover of Beautiful Things, believing that his adopted son had—— stolen the little treasure? If so, then the potter was knowing even greater sorrow, and he was carrying even an angrier mind against his new son.

The boy strove to push the thought away, at the same time telling himself that, even at the risk of meeting the pock-marked one, even at the risk of being thrown into prison, he, Fen, must return the little red dragon.

Quickly retracing his steps, the boy found the country-man feeding his pony. "Respected Sir," he murmured, bowing low, "would you permit me to ride in your cart tomorrow when you again carry melons to Hankow? Heaven wills it, Sir, for in my pocket lies a charm piece, which I carried away without intention. It belongs not to me, but to an honorable old one."

"I go no more to Hankow until spring," replied the farmer, "when I carry early peaches to the gates of the rich. Therefore, young son, you must journey on foot. The distance from my poor farm, eastward to the city, is thirty-six li."

Thirty-six li! How long would it take him to cover the distance on a lame foot? But——even though it required a full moon's time of trudging over hills and through swamp lands, the little red dragon must be returned. But, before he slept this night, the jade charm piece must be hidden under the lining of his outer coat. For sewing the treasure into a place of safe keeping, he would need a length of stout thread. But where in this strange country would he find such a thing?

With fresh determination, young Fen set out once again for the house of Win. The first shy star of evening now appeared in the west. Bats were darting. Crickets called.

All at once a countryman, on his way home from a village, passed along the road. He was singing and from his belt swung a bottle of good soy sauce. On what warm food would the sauce be used this night? pondered the boy, his spirit drooping.

Presently the countryman called to young Fen, "*Peng on a?*" (Is all well with you?)

Limping One longed to cry out after the fellow who had gone on his way singing, "All is *not* well with me, O Countryman!"

Finally, he came to a mud hut with a thatched roof. As he neared the low dwelling, the boy could hear a woman singing a melody tender as a Soochow lullaby. Kind hearts must live in the mean hut, the boy decided, his spirit lifting.

The next moment he was asking himself: with what good food might their eating bowls be filled this night? He could picture them welling over with hot cabbage topped by bits of pork. Impulsively his hand flew out. He rapped on the door.

It was opened by an old woman with white hair. "You are a stranger," she declared. "What do you wish?"

"I——I go to Hankow to return a——charm piece, Lao Po Po," (grandmother) "but first I offer the strength of my arms for a length of stout thread and a corner on your mud floor in which to lie this night."

The old woman turned to thrust a handful of field grass

into a clay stove, at the same time demanding, "For what
do you need thread, White Face?"

Sudden panic chilled the heart of young Fen. Would
Lao Po Po take from him the little red dragon in payment
for a length of thread? The Wins appeared to be poor
folk, and the jade dragon would bring silver coins if sold
to a dealer in rare trinkets.

"I would look upon the charm piece," declared the old
woman.

Ai-ya! His thoughts in a whirl, the boy closed his fingers
over the treasure.

"I would look upon it!" repeated the woman.

While fear clutched at his heart, slowly, reluctantly,
young Fen laid the bit of jade in the woman's hand.

As he waited, breathless, she studied the charm piece,
her old eyes brightening. Finally the woman spoke, "Because the dragon of jade belongs to a worthy old one, you
are bound by honor to return it, my son, though you must
walk barefoot over rocky paths to do so." She placed the
carved red stone in the boy's waiting hand. Again, his
fingers closed over it protectingly.

"What can you do with your arms?" asked an old man,
glancing up from his knitting.

"Anything, Grandfather," vowed the boy.

"Then tomorrow you shall dig turnips in my field. The
wars have taken my sons, and an evil spirit has placed a

weakness in my body. Therefore, I need the strength of young arms."

The old man turned to a woman who was tucking her baby into its bamboo cradle and said, "Prepare the boy a towel wrung out of hot water that he may wipe his face and hands. Then give him a bowl of tea and a cake of bean curd. After he has eaten and drunk, let him lie the night on a sack of bamboo shavings. Tomorrow, if the youth works as well as he talks, he shall have a bowl of evening rice, as well as a length of thread."

CHAPTER 6

The next morning, at the Hour of the Hare, young Fen set out toward Win's field. His hunger was now like a clutching hand beneath his girdle. He reached for the sugared plum, thrusting it whole into his mouth. Biting into the brown goodness, he chewed slowly, striving to make it last.

As he dug turnips in the faint light of dawn, Limping One again knew a fine pride in his arms. By their strength he could earn food and places to sleep while making his journey back to Hankow.

As the sun climbed high, blisters formed on the boy's hands. He gazed at them troubled, remembering again the term, "beauty-making fingers," once used by his foster father. The potter had promised that he, young Fen, would one day be chosen to make a ceremonial urn. He had hinted that his new son *might* be allowed to paint upon

the urn the heaven-sent Crane-Moon-And-Plum-Tree design; lastly, perhaps carry the urn to the temple beyond the moon gate————

Ai-ya! Such an opportunity——perhaps to bring honor to the House of Chang——was now gone, for he, Fen, had become a farmer's helper with blistered hands. Perhaps Meng, the oldest apprentice, who possessed skill in tracing designs, would in time be made son of the House. At the thought, Limping One murmured, "I carry a small heart." He pushed yet another barrow of turnips across the field.

The morning hours passed slowly, bringing a bowl of tea, as well as a handful of melon seeds at midday. When the sun set, young Fen's hands were both red and swollen when the old grandmother placed in them a bowl of evening rice. As he held the bowl with a fierce eagerness tight against him, inhaling the warm moist breath of the food and savoring its goodness on his tongue, the boy wondered and wondered again if Win, the farmer, would remember his promise about the length of thread.

When the evening candle was lit, the old man cut thread from a skein, at the same time remarking, "It would be wisdom to sew the dragon of jade into your girdle lest misfortune befall your outer jacket on the way to Hankow."

The next morning, young Fen began to journey eastward. At a turning in the road he came upon a shrine built to Kwan Yin, Goddess of Mercy and Pity. The boy gazed wistfully at the little image, whose face was tenderly serene and beautiful as she gazed down upon him. His heart beating high, he was certain that the gentle goddess was leaning toward him ever so slightly as though awaiting his prayer.

Well the boy knew that no whispered plea was too timid or too stumbling for her listening ears to understand. In dismay, however, he realized that he had no incense with which to honor the goddess of the gentle heart. So he could make only the customary kowtow before the shrine. Dropping to his knees, Limping One, like a reed in the wind, swayed rhythmically forth and back, at the same time murmuring, "O Lady-Who-Listens-To-Prayers, have the goodness to open the way across rocky trails and around paddy fields, and over bridges, for I would carry the little red dragon to the honorable Chang in the city of Hankow!"

Days passed and young Fen was making slow progress toward the city gates. One morning he passed a country-man who was driving a pair of buffaloes hitched tandem to a plough. How good it would be to lie for an hour on the edge of the field and watch the farmer till his land! However, he dared not stop merely to rest, but only to work for rice and tea. "O Elder Brother!" the boy called to the man. "Will you tell me a thing? How many li must I yet travel to reach the gates of Hankow?"

"As the crane flies, the distance from my unworthy farm is ten li."

"Ten li!" repeated the boy in sharp dismay, for already his sandals had commenced to break.

More days passed while young Fen stopped to earn rice and tea by blowing bellows for a village welder. Finally the man sent the boy on his way with two wheaten cakes tucked into his sleeve pocket.

As he journeyed, his hand often crept to his girdle into which the little red dragon had been carefully sewed. At the feel of it, the boy's step quickened but at the same time, dread stole into his heart. How would the potter receive him? the boy asked himself over and over again. Would the man with a blue button on his cap be lurking in a byway, ready to pounce upon him?

With his strong arms and skilled fingers, Chang Fen had earned his rice and tea for nearly half a moon's time by digging in fields, by cutting vegetables for drying, by tending goats. For two days he had made slabs of ink, thus staining his calloused hands with the soot of sesamum oil until they were black as ebony. In every low mud hut the boy had found magic at work, which transformed skeins of silk, as well as bamboo, rice paper, wood and clay into things of beauty.

Each night, when recalling the potter's words, "beauty-making fingers," Fen hid his rough and blackened hands behind him. Never, he was certain, could they now create beauty of any kind. Least of all, beauty lovely enough for temple use. At the thought, he again whispered to himself, *"I carry a small heart."*

The days grew colder. One morning the boy came to the Village of Tall Pine Trees. A little stream ran there, and a woman was beating clothes on its bank. "I wish to know a thing, Respected Mother," he said, bowing before the woman. "How many li must I yet travel to reach the city of Hankow?"

"Six li, Little Brother with broken sandals, and the path from this village is steep. May the winds blow not against you!"

It was again morning and the time was the middle of the tenth moon. Frozen Dew now lay across the fields, and clouds, pale as steamed rice, were moving down the sky. As young Fen approached a village, he met a white-haired man who was airing a pet bird on his arm. The boy's words stumbled from weariness when he asked, "W-will you tell me, Old Head, how—how many li stretch before me to the gates of Hankow?"

"Two li, you with no sandals," replied the man. "But the way is rough. May the God-of-Journeys watch over you, Lame One, and may you reach the city gates before the Wintry Breath of the Dragon (snow) covers your path!"

CHAPTER 7

At a turning in the steep path, Chang Fen stopped to earn midday rice and tea by carrying bundles of dry mountain grass for a villager's clay stove. Toward evening of the same day, the boy could see, rising ahead of him, the dust-colored walls of Hankow! Kwan Yin, the Lady-Who-Listens-To-Prayers, as well as the God-of-Journeys, *had* watched over him, young Fen told himself in wan triumph, for the little red dragon still lay secure within his girdle, and no one had taken from him his good padded coat.

He must crouch in the shadow of the city wall until darkness came, and then travel only through dim lanes. In this manner, the boy reasoned, he might avoid capture by the man with a blue button on his cap. At thought of him, panic again chilled the heart of young Fen. But, even at the risk of capture, he must cross the city to Chang's door.

This might require two days without rice and tea, as well as two nights of scuttling through byways.

While the tinkling gong of a food seller rang faintly, Limping One pulled his outer coat high about his neck and sat by the ancient brick wall to await darkness. His hand cupped protectingly over the jade charm piece, sewed within his girdle, the boy fell asleep to the droning voice of a chrysanthemum vender, "Lai, mei hua'rh! Lai, mei hua-rh!" (Come, buy flowers!)

A night and two days had passed, and it was again the hour of evening rice. Chang Fen had finally reached Embroidery Makers' Lane with its foot-passengers, its rickshas, its venders, its horns and tinkling bells. The boy, hunching low, scurried from one shadowed doorway to another, striving to lose himself in the milling crowds. Only a few steps now lay between him and Pottery-Making Street! Perhaps, mused the boy, Honorable Chang would understand that he, young Fen, was nearly falling with hunger. Who could tell? The potter then might lay down his angry heart long enough to provide a bowl of evening rice.

The next moment a hand dropped on the boy's shoulder, and a voice of authority spoke against his ear. "This time, Lame Foot, you shall not escape!"

For a moment, Chang Fen stood as a thing frozen against the earth. Forcing himself, he turned his head slowly, slowly, and then summoning all his courage, he lifted his eyes, only to look into the face of the pock-marked one. *Ai-ya!* The word struggled in the boy's throat, but his lips made no sound as the man's grasp tightened upon him. For this, had he endured half a moon of hunger and spirit-breaking work? To this end, had he slept on mud floors and walked barefoot over rocky trails? Surely all was now lost! Of a certainty, Kwan Yin, as well as the God-of-Journeys, had forsaken him, the boy told himself. Never as now had he needed their protection. In desperation, he whispered a swift frantic plea to the gods for help.

At the same moment, there was a commotion in the narrow streetway, for, at a little distance, there sounded the deep-throated bells of a camel train. This meant, Chang Fen knew, that a loaded caravan of goods was passing through Hankow. Presently, the camels swung into Embroidery-Makers' Lane. At the clang of their bells, which caused a deafening blare in the narrow street, all vendors, as well as the gaping crowd, pressed close to walls and doorways. The caravan with its heavy packs lumbered on its way.

Limping One felt the hand on his shoulder relax. At the same moment, a daring thought came to him. Should he make a dash, striving to bolt between the legs of a camel? As if in answer to the question, high courage came flooding into the boy's heart, for he was certain that, from some far-distant place, the God-of-Journeys was smiling and nod-

ding his head as though saying, "He who dares nót gains
nothing, young son. So pluck up your heart, and then run
swift as a badger between the legs of a camel. *Hasten!*"

Fleet as a shuttle-cock whirling through the air, Chang
Fen appeared to throw himself at the camel train, at the
same time leaving his padded coat in the grasp of the pock-
marked one.

As the boy stumbled, there were shrill cries, "Ngoi!
Ngoi!" (Foolish one!) "Would you break your bones?"

Ai-ya! His lame foot had tricked him! for he now fell
and then rolled beneath the caravan. He had been thumped
by a hoof, his trousers were torn, his face bleeding, when
kindly hands dragged him to his feet on the other side of
Embroidery-Makers' Lane. Again, arose the cry, "Ngoi!"

Without even hearing the shrill word, Limping One,
urged on by the fear of recapture, darted blindly past Bell-
Makers' Way. As darkness came on, he scuttled into
Pottery-Making Street. Now he stood at Chang's door.
Though, at last, he had reached the end of his long journey,
he dared not enter the shop, young Fen told his thundering
heart, for——*how would the potter receive him?*

All at once he was longing desperately to run back over
the city byways, through the tall gates and then into the
country, there to hide under cover of the deepening night.
But all at once, over the noises of the street, the boy seemed
again to hear the words, "He who dares not gains nothing,

young son." Tearing the little red dragon from his girdle, Limping One opened the door of the shop.

Gathering all his courage, he forced his body step by step into the inner room, where Meng was placing a bowl of evening rice on the square red table before Chang. The next moment, Fen, with trembling hand, laid the dragon of jade on the edge of the table, murmuring, "H-honorable One, the——the charm piece——I-I return it——"

Without a word, Chang slipped the trinket into his sleeve pocket. He then arose slowly, slowly, appearing to the youth to grow tall as a pine tree. Then he seized young Fen by the shoulders. "Come with me," he commanded, at the same time snatching up the vegetable oil lamp. "Come!"

The boy found himself being pushed from the inner room and then into the garden. Dazed, frightened, trembling, he watched as Chang, by the glow of the lamp, removed bricks from the moist earth of a flower bed. Beneath the bricks, Limping One could see huge footprints leading to the mud wall.

"My son——Son of my House," murmured Chang, "here, in your well-watered garden, are the footprints of a prowler."

But Limping One heard only the words, "My son." In wonder, he repeated them under his breath. Never before had they seemed so noble or of such high worth, for Chang had again called him by these words! This told that no one, by the law of adoption, had been put into his place during his absence! This told also that there was still a chance that he, Fen, might yet be chosen to copy the sacred design. There was *still* a chance that he might yet bring honor to the revered House of Chang———!

"The prowler," continued Chang, "was no doubt one of the city's common fuel thieves who came with his sack, hunting for bricks of charcoal. A sandal, which fits the footprints, I found here in the garden the morning after you left my house. Also——" Chang dropped his voice to a whisper, "over the ninth flagstone, I found your bed mat and *pu-gai*. After that it was not difficult to piece together the story that convinced me of your innocence and proved your courage.

"Each day, for half a moon's time," Chang added, "I have laid down my heart for you, deploring my quick judgment. Moreover, in grief I have searched for you. Placards, offering reward for your safe return, I had posted in the market places and on roadways. In addition, I have employed an *om chai** who wears, for high service, the blue button awarded him by the Emperor. I have offered the respected *om chai* twelve taels in pure silver, hoping that he might find and bring you back to me."

His hand on the boy's shoulder, Chang was now smiling and calling into the shop to Chi, who was peering through the latticed window, "Ho there, Chi! Stop gaping, and put

* Under-cover policeman.

down your eating bowl, for tonight we shall all feast! Go
at once to the Isle of Pleasures Restaurant and tell Lo,
the worthy proprietor, that the son, who was lost to the
lowly House of Chang for half a moon's time, has returned.
Tell Lo to prepare a tray with stuffed duck, bamboo shoots,
sweetened eggs, red sugar cakes, and a savory soup for
washing down the meal.

"Furthermore, before you sleep go to Wu, the Tailor
on Garment-Making Way, and tell him that the son of
Chang has returned. Order Wu to bring rolls of cloth that
I may choose from them, for my son must be measured
for new garments. When you return, spread the lacquered
table with the green dragon cloth, for, though it is not yet
winter, spring has come to my old heart!"

Listening, wondering, rejoicing over the words that the
potter had spoken, Chang Fen stood as one in a dream, and
again he thought how Chang, a moment ago, had called
him——son! Moreover, he was planning to spread before
him the food of a mandarin! To provide new clothes for
him. Even the man with a blue button on his cap had not
been one to be feared! Instead, from the beginning, he had
been a kind of—— friend, whose intention had been to
bring him, Fen, back to the house of his father.

His head spinning in bewilderment over these strange
good ways of heaven, the boy, who had not eaten for two
days, fell in a faint at Chang's feet.

Quickly, the potter lifted his son, and with great strides

carried him to his good tile bed. Tenderly, he bent over young Fen, and droned a charm that was old as the first written records of China. The charm, which had been used with faith down the centuries, was said to possess powers for driving sickness from the body, as well as grief from the spirit.

The ancient charm had no doubt done its good work, for presently Chang Fen opened his eyes, and a faint smile tilted his lips. He arose and stood, remembering quickly to hide his blackened and calloused hands behind him, for surely the potter, Lover of Beautiful Things, would be offended by such ugliness.

Chang held a cup of warm rice gruel to the boy's lips, gazing down at him in compassion as he drank it. "My son," he murmured, "my chosen son, nowhere in the Flowery Kingdom would I have recognized you in your soiled and torn clothes, which smell of the sheep pen. Nor would I have recognized you in the whiteness and thinness of your face; but——" reaching for the boy's hands, the potter, with force, drew them into the light. "But," he continued, "anywhere in the Flowery Kingdom I would have known thee by thy beauty-making fingers. Thy hands tell thy story! In a moon's time, however, they will whiten. *Ai!* In a single moon's time they will soften, ready for holding the honorable white kaolin! Then——for two winters and two summers you shall practice again with the potter's wheel."

At the promise, Chang Fen's eyes glistened, and in fancy he could again hear the murmur of the beloved wheel, which to him always seemed like the whirring of cranes' wings against the sky.

As Chi spread the feast, the potter drew the little red dragon from his sleeve pocket. Rubbing his thumb over the smooth bit of jade, he murmured dreamily, "In your sixteenth summer, you shall try your skill at fashioning a ceremonial urn of white kaolin. You shall bake the urn to the color of an autumn peach, and you shall then paint upon it the heaven-sent Crane-Moon-And-Plum-Tree design, for in every generation in the House of Chang a youth is appointed for this work. If you can perform each step without flaw, my son, you may then wrap the urn in a brocaded gift cloth, and carry it to the temple beyond the moon gate. There you shall offer it humbly as a ceremonial piece for holding the honorable joss sticks."

Scarcely daring to breathe, young Fen listened in wonderment to Chang's words, and a joyous singing set up in his heart, for, beneath the calloused and blackened surface, his revered father could still vision beauty-making fingers! So, after all, he, Chang Fen, *would* be chosen to create beauty! At the mere thought, the singing in the boy's heart seemed to ring like the notes of temple bells, for his arms and fingers might yet help him bring honor to the respected House of Chang.

The potter now placed the little red dragon in the boy's roughened hands, whispering, "My Jade One I give to you, Son of my House. Always it has brought me good luck. Likewise, it should bring good luck to you."

The little red dragon to be his very own! In his amazement, Chang Fen could neither move nor speak. His eyes glowing like feast-day candles, he cradled in his hands the treasure of jade. It was a charm piece! Would it put a working magic into his fingers?

The boy tried to think of beautiful words, shining words, that would tell of his happiness. "Respected Sir,——" he began, bowing his head three times to the floor. But he found that he possessed no words that could in any way tell his feeling. "Honorable One——" he began again, while Chang waited, eyes twinkling. "Thrice Revered

One," murmured the boy. "I——my heart is——is no longer small——"

The night watchman, again threading his way through the dark, struck his musical gong, and called lustily, "It is the Hour of the Dog, and all is well on Pottery-Making Street."

Dat